vincent

The Cows Are Going to Paris

THE COWS ARE GOING TO PARIS

TO PARIS

by DAVID KIRBY & ALLEN WOODMAN
Illustrated by CHRIS L. DEMAREST

BOYDS MILLS PRESS

For Barbara and Jane and Kent—D.K. AND A.W.
For Laura and Sarah—C.D.

Text copyright © 1991 by David Kirby and Allen Woodman
Illustrations copyright © 1991 by Chris L. Demarest

Published by Caroline House
Boyds Mills Press, Inc.
A Highlights Company
910 Church Street
Honesdale, Pennsylvania 18431
Printed in Hong Kong
First edition, 1991
Distributed by St. Martin's Press

Book designed by Joy Chu

Publisher Cataloging-in-Publication Data
Kirby, David.
The cows are going to Paris/by David Kirby and Allen Woodman: illustrated
by Chris L. Demarest.
    32p. : ill.; cm.
Summary: A delightful picture book of the day a herd of cows leaves the pasture
and boards the train for Paris. The cows dress up in clothes and royally tour the city
before returning home.
ISBN 1-878093-11-8
1. Cows—Stories—Juvenile Literature. 2. Picture-books—Juvenile Literature.
[1. Cows—Stories. 2. Picture-books.] I. Woodman, Allen. II. Demarest, Chris L., ill.
III. Title.
813.54-dc20   [E]   1991
LC Card Number 90-85733

10 9 8 7 6 5 4 3

The cows have grown tired of the fields. The cows are going to Paris.

When the cows board the train at Fontainebleau, the people are frightened and run out into the pastures and meadows and chew grass.

The cows are delighted to be on the train.

One cow prankster sticks her head out of the window and shouts "M-m-moo!" and "M-m-m-ooo!" at passing farmers.

The people left the train in such haste that they forgot to take their suitcases.

The cows dress up in their borrowed clothes.

The cows admire their slipper-shod hoofs. They try to squeeze their full haunches into fashionable dresses and trousers. It had never occurred to them what fun it could be to wear French berets and other fanciful hats.

In Paris the cows say "Bonjour!" to everyone they meet. The word pleases them. It tickles their mouths to say anything other than "moo."

The cows take the elevators to the top of the tower. All of Paris lies below them like a dream of a toy city.

Back on the ground, the cows purchase little metal Eiffel Towers in the souvenir shops.

Then the cows decide they are hungry. The cows had always heard that in Paris dogs are allowed in restaurants, so they think there will be no problem about cows.

The cows head straight for a restaurant called Maxim's. The maitre d' shouts "How now! How now!" and is so wonderstruck by the costumed cows coming through the doorway that he gives them the best seats in the dining room.

The chef prepares a special dish for them called *casserole de l'herbe*. The cows assure him that it tastes every bit as good as the fresh grass of the countryside.

After eating, the cows spend some time hoofing about the art exhibits at the Louvre museum. Leonardo da Vinci's *Mona Lisa* makes them all smile.

Then the cows go shopping at the Galeries Lafayette. The cows browse through all of the ten floors of the department store.

One cow is even sprayed with a sample of perfume. The smell of it reminds the cows of the sweet fragrance of wild flowers.

Meanwhile, the people from the train have made themselves comfortable under the trees. The diet of the cows is nourishing and unrefined, and somehow it seems natural to stand in small groups for hours, saying nothing.

Indeed, when the cows return to the fields and meadows, the people will not get back on board the train. They must be prodded before they enter the cars.

Finally, the cows scatter their souvenir Eiffel Towers about the pasture. They happily imagine the surprise of the farmers when they find the small treasures hidden in the tall, lush grass.

Having been to the city, the cows see that there is something wonderful about visiting a new place. But they know that there is something just as fine about coming home.